The New Kid
from the
Black Lagoon

by Mike Thaler · pictures by Jared Lee

SCHOLASTIC INC.

New York   Toronto   London   Auckland   Sydney
Mexico City   New Delhi   Hong Kong   Buenos Aires

visit us at www.abdopublishing.com

Reinforced library bound edition published in 2012 by Spotlight, a division of the ABDO Group, PO Box 398166, Minneapolis, MN 55439. Spotlight produces high-quality reinforced library bound editions for schools and libraries. Published by agreement with Scholastic Inc.

Printed in the United States of America, North Mankato, Minnesota.
102011
012012

 This book contains at least 10% recycled materials.

For Hannah Joy, the new kid on our block.
—M.T.

To all the new kids who face a new school, new classmates,
new challenges, new experiences, new friends,
and new rewards.
—J.L.

Text copyright © 2004 by Mike Thaler. Illustrations copyright © 2004 by Jared D. Lee Studio, Inc.
All rights reserved. Published by Scholastic Inc. SCHOLASTIC and associated
logos are trademarks and/or registered trademarks of Scholastic Inc.

Library of Congress Cataloging-in-Publication Data

This book was previously cataloged with the following information:

Thaler, Mike, 1936-
  The new kid from the black lagoon / by Mike Thaler ; pictures by Jared Lee.
    p. cm.
[1. School children—Juvenile fiction. 2. Schools—Juvenile fiction. 3. School children—Juvenile fiction.]
PZ7.T3 New 2004
[E}-dc22
                                                    2004555573

ISBN 978-1-59961-956-9 (reinforced library edition)

Spotlight

All Spotlight books are reinforced library bindings
and manufactured in the United States of America.

Mrs. Green says that we're getting a new kid in our class.

His name is Xu, and he comes from far away.

"Miami?" asks the class.

"Farther," answers Mrs. Green.

"Moscow?" we ask.

"Farther," she says.

"Mars!" I shout out.

Mrs. Green just smiles.

On the bus home, I begin to wonder what the new kid will look like.
If he's from Mars, he'll probably be pretty weird. Eric thinks he'll
have a tiny head with eyes on stalks and a nose like a pickle.

Derek thinks he'll have purple eyebrows,
green antennae, and blue skin.

Maybe he won't have skin at all! Maybe he'll have Velcro, and he'll stick to everything.

Maybe he'll be a giant chicken, or a bionic turnip with three arms and four legs. If he is, then I want him on *my* basketball team.

Then again, he could have fins for fingers and tentacles for toes.

I just hope he's friendly.

Randy says maybe he's coming to take over the world.

He'll have laser breath and radioactive B.O.

Or worse, maybe he'll be a body *snacker*.

And when he's a-munching, we'll be luncheon.

 Freddy thinks that he'll just eat Mars Bars, marz-ipan, and Martian-mallows.

I hope that he'll be a buddy, and not a bully.

 I wonder if he'll wear clothes or run around naked.

I wonder if he ever goes to the bathroom.

I wonder how he got here. Maybe in a flying saucer or a flying cup?

I bet it's a Model Tea or a Tea-Bird. I wonder if he'll give us a ride.

Maybe he'll take us home for a sleepover party . . . on Mars! He'll probably have to ask his mom and dad. I wonder what *they're* like.

Well, I guess I'll just have to wait for tomorrow and see.

 "Class, I'd like you to meet Xu Ping, who's flown here all the way from China," says Mrs. Green.

"Sit down," I say. "You must be very tired."

"Just my arms." Xu Ping smiles, and he gives me a high five.

Then he gives us all chopsticks and invites us to come to his
mom and dad's new restaurant for dinner.

He's cool, but I'm taking a fork just in case.